The Hu

Mull

The Humorous Stories
of
Mulla Nasrudin

Rupa & Co

First in Rupa Paperback 2001
Fourth impression 2003

Published by

Rupa • Co

7/16, Ansari Road, Daryaganj,
New Delhi 110 002

Sales Centres:

Allahabad Bangalore Chandigarh Chennai
Dehradun Hyderabad Jaipur Kathmandu
Kolkata Ludhiana Mumbai Pune

ISBN 81-7167-558-1

Typeset Copyright © Rupa & Co. 2001

Typeset by
Nikita Overseas Pvt Ltd, 19 A, Ansari Road,
New Delhi 110 002

Printed in India by
Saurabh Print-O-Pack, A-16, Sector 4,
Noida 201 301

Contents

Doctor Nasrudin

Nasrudin was visiting a sick friend when the doctor arrived to examine the patient. The doctor looked at the patient's tongue and said, "You have been eating too many apples. If you want to get rid of that stomach-ache you must stop eating apples."

The patient was amazed that the doctor knew what he had been eating. Nasrudin followed the doctor out of the room and asked him, "Doctor, please tell me how you did that!"

"It's easy. When I sat down to examine him, I saw a pile of eaten apple-cores under the man's bed. It was easy to guess that the stomach-ache was because of that."

Nasrudin was impressed and thanked the doctor before leaving.

One day Nasrudin went to visit another friend of his. The friend's wife answered the door and said, "He is not well. Please come another day."

But Nasrudin stayed at the door. "What is the matter with him? Maybe I can cure him. I know a few of the doctor's secrets," he boasted.

"Oh no! He needs a doctor. What do you know about curing stomach-aches?"

"Stomach-aches!" exclaimed Nasrudin. "Those are my area of specialty. Let me in. I can cure him."

The wife was tired of arguing and let him in. Nasrudin went up to where the patient lay groaning and peeped under the bed. Then he stood up and announced, "This man is fine. But why has he been eating all those shoes? Stop eating shoes and you will be cured instantly."

The Missing Keys

It was late and Nasrudin was down on all fours on the street in front of his house. It looked like he was searching for something.

"What are you looking for?" people asked him.

"I have lost my keys," he answered. Some men bent down to assist him in the search. They looked everywhere, but could not find the missing keys.

Finally, growing tired, one of the men asked him, "Where exactly did you drop them?"

"Inside my house."

"But then why are you looking over here?"

"Obviously it is easier to look for them over here! There is more light here than inside my house!"

A Thief in the House

One night Nasrudin was sitting on the street outside his house. He suddenly saw a burglar entering his house from a side window. The burglar did not see Nasrudin in the dark. The Mulla was scared to go and fight the thief. He watched as the thief loaded almost all his possessions onto a donkey and set off. Nasrudin ran into his house, picked up a blanket and began following the thief. Soon the thief reached his own house and began to unload the donkey. Nasrudin went into the man's house quietly and pretended to go to sleep under his blanket.

Soon the thief came in and asked, "What do you think you are doing in my house?"

"*Your* house?" asked Nasrudin. "I thought you were shifting houses for *me*!"

Help the Needy

One day Nasrudin went to a neighbour of his and said, "I am collecting money to help a needy man who cannot pay off his debts. Will you please donate some money?"

"That is good work you are doing Nasrudin," said the neighbour as he gave Nasrudin some money. "Who is this needy man you are helping?"

"Its me!" said Nasrudin, as he walked off quickly.

After a few weeks he came back to the neighbour with the same request: "Please contribute some money so that a needy man can pay off his debts."

"You can't fool me twice Nasrudin. The money is for you. I am sure of it."

"I swear. I am not collecting the money to pay off my debts," said Nasrudin seriously.

"Oh, all right! Here you are," said the

neighbour as he handed Nasrudin some money.

"Thank you. You are a good man."

"But how come you are doing good for another man?" asked the neighbour.

"Well, you see, in this case the needy man is one who owes *me* some money!"

Sweet and Salty

One day Nasrudin and a friend stopped at a little restaurant. They were both very thirsty and decided to share a glass of milk. When the milk came, the friend suggested that Nasrudin drink half first.

"I have got a little sugar with me," said the friend, "but it is just enough for me. So after you have drunk your half I will add the sugar to my half."

"Why don't you add it now?" Nasrudin said. "I will only drink my half."

"No, no. This little bit of sugar cannot sweeten a full glass of milk," said the man.

So Nasrudin went and got some salt from the kitchen.

"Well then," he said. "You can sweeten your half later. But I will have my half after adding this salt to it."

A Good Tip

One day Nasrudin went to a massage parlour. The attendants at the parlour were very good at giving relaxing massages to the customers. But when they saw Nasrudin's simple clothes and ordinary appearance they paid him very little attention. They thought he was a poor man. They were used to massaging rich men who gave a big tip.

When he left, Nasrudin tipped them one gold coin each. They were very surprised at his generosity, as he did not look rich. Perhaps, they thought, if they had given him a better massage he might have left a bigger tip.

The next week Nasrudin returned to the parlour. This time the attendants looked after him very well. They went out of their way to make him comfortable and treated him like a king. They massaged him with special scented oil till he smelt lovely. When he was leaving,

Nasrudin gave each attendant the smallest possible coin as a tip.

The men looked very upset, and before they could say anything, Nasrudin said, "This is for last time. And the gold coins were for this time!"

The Lost Turban

Nasrudin had lost a very beautiful and expensive turban. But he did not seem to be very upset about it.

"Don't you miss your turban, Nasrudin?" someone asked him.

"Oh, I am sure someone will find it," said the Mulla cheerfully. "I am promising a reward of one silver piece."

"Do you think anyone will return a turban that cost almost a hundred silver pieces for a reward of one piece of silver?" asked the man.

"Do you think I did not think of that already? I have announced that I have lost an old, cheap turban. That is very different from what the real turban is like."

Candle-light

It was mid-winter. The whole village was covered in snow. A few of Nasrudin's friends made a bet with him. They said that he would not be able to spend an entire night alone on the top of a nearby mountain in the freezing cold. The Mulla bet them that he could. He set off for the mountain that night with a book and a candle. It was bitterly cold that night and he almost froze to death.

The next morning, the frostbitten Mulla went around to collect his money from the men.

"You mean you had nothing that kept you warm at night and you still survived?" they asked disbelievingly.

"Honestly," swore the Mulla. "All I had were a book to read and a candle to provide the necessary light."

"But that candle must have kept you warm as well. The bet is off." In this way they wriggled out of paying Nasrudin any money.

After a few weeks the Mulla invited all those men to his house for a meal, promising them delicious food. They arrived right on time, ready to eat. Most of them had skipped breakfast so that they could eat more. But Nasrudin kept them waiting, saying that the food was not cooked yet. After two hours the guests were really hungry. They complained loudly that Nasrudin was a bad host.

"Perhaps we should go take a look at the food while it's cooking," suggested Nasrudin. They all followed him into the kitchen and saw a huge vessel, cooking over the flame of just one small candle. No wonder the food wasn't cooked. They all turned and looked at the Mulla for an explanation.

"Hmm... it's not ready yet. It has been cooking since yesterday. I wonder what's wrong," mused the Mulla. "If a candle can keep a man warm in the snow, surely it can cook food too!"

Brave Nasrudin

One day, in the teahouse of the village, a group of soldiers were narrating stories of bravery during battles they had fought. The fascinated villagers listened to each story with open mouths and wide eyes. There were tales of attacks, killings and victories. At the end of each story there was loud clapping. The soldiers were enjoying telling their stories to such an enthusiastic audience.

Suddenly, Nasrudin interrupted them by saying, "That reminds me of what I once did."

Everyone turned to look at him. He had never been a soldier. But Nasrudin was determined to tell his story.

"Once I cut off the leg of an enemy soldier and showed it to the king. I got a handsome reward."

The villagers were impressed at this unexpected tale of bravery from Nasrudin.

The captain of the soldiers said, "You should have cut off his head! That would have been better and you might have got a bigger reward."

"How could I have done that?" asked Nasrudin. "Someone had already cut off his head by the time I got to him!"

Quick Work

Nasrudin was working for a rich man. The man could not bear Nasrudin's way of working. One day, Nasrudin went to the market three times to buy three eggs. Each time, he bought one egg because he was scared that they would break.

Finally, the rich man lost his patience. "Nasrudin, learn to save time! You should do more than one thing at a time."

Nasrudin promised to try harder.

One day, the man fell ill. He was in great pain. He asked Nasrudin to call the doctor. After a while, Nasrudin returned. He led the doctor to his master's room and said, "Here is the doctor. The others are waiting outside."

"What do you mean 'others', Nasrudin?" gasped the man.

"Master, I have brought the chemist to provide the medicines that the doctor

prescribes. I have brought the coal-seller in case we need more coal to make a bigger fire to keep you warm. I have brought the priest to pray for your recovery. And just in case none of that works, I have brought the coffin-maker to measure you for your coffin."

The Donkey who Tried to be Clever

One day the Mulla was taking his donkey to the market to sell some salt. The poor donkey huffed and puffed under the weight of all the salt that he was carrying. As they crossed through a stream the tired animal lost its balance and stumbled into the water. Immediately all the salt dissolved and the donkey's burden was gone. While the donkey was relieved, Nasrudin was very upset.

Another day, he led the donkey towards the stream. This time they were taking cotton wool to the market. The donkey decided to be clever. It twisted sideways and lay down in the water. All the wool got soaked through and the burden became twice as heavy. The poor donkey had a hard time making it all the way till the market.

"Ha!" laughed the Mulla. "You thought you could take it easy *every* time, didn't you?"

Silence is Golden

Several people were sitting and meditating in the mosque. Nasrudin was also praying there. As a rule, nobody spoke at this time because it disturbed the concentration of the others. Suddenly, one man spoke in the silence: "I think I have left the fire burning in my house by mistake."

The man next to him was disturbed and said, "Now you have broken the silence and your prayer is incomplete. You must start again."

"You have done the same thing," added the man sitting behind him.

Nasrudin was laughing to himself at the foolishness of these men who had all broken their silence. "I am the only one who has remained silent," he said out loud.

The Early Bird

Nasrudin's father was trying to persuade Nasrudin to wake up early each morning. "But why, Father?" asked the sleepy Nasrudin.

"It is a good habit. It might bring you luck. You know, once I went for a walk at dawn and found a sack of gold on the street. It must have fallen from someone's cart."

"But it could have been left there the previous night," argued Nasrudin.

"No, no. The night before I had not seen it when I walked down that road."

"Well then,' said Nasrudin. "It is not lucky for everyone to be up and about early in the morning. The man who lost that gold must have woken up even earlier than you." And Nasrudin went back to sleep.

Blessings from God

It was raining cats and dogs. Aga Akil, a religious man with whom Nasrudin had had many arguments, was caught in the rain and started running for shelter.

"Shame on you. This is God's blessing on us from heaven and you are showing it disrespect by running from it!" shouted the Mulla when he saw the sight.

The Aga didn't want others to think that he was not religious. So he mumbled, "I never thought of it like that before." He slowed down and reached home dripping wet.

A little later he was sitting at his window, wrapped in a blanket, because he had caught a cold. Suddenly he saw Nasrudin running at top speed towards a nearby shelter. "I thought—Aaa-aaa-tishhooo—this was a blessing from God, Mulla. Why then are you running from it?" the Aga shouted.

"Of course it is God's blessing," replied Nasrudin over the sound of the rain. "Naturally I do not want to be rude to God by putting my feet on it!"

Fresh *Halwa*

One day Nasrudin persuaded his wife to cook *halwa*, which was a great favourite of his. Soon a plate of steaming hot, delicious *halwa* was sitting before the Mulla. He ate the lion's share of it. Only a little was left and his wife forced him to save it for the next day.

In the middle of the night, Nasrudin shook his sleeping wife awake.

"I just had a really interesting thought!"

"What?" asked his wife, rubbing her eyes sleepily.

"It is really a great idea!" said Nasrudin, almost to himself.

"What is it?" asked his wife.

"Never mind. Go back to sleep."

But now his wife was wide-awake and very curious.

"Tell me what it is!" she insisted.

"I will tell you if you bring me the rest of the *halwa* from the kitchen."

So the wife brought it all for him on a plate and he ate it greedily as she watched. When he had finished licking the plate clean, she could bear it no more.

"What was your interesting thought?" she asked.

"I thought that I should eat all the *halwa* while it is still fresh instead of eating it stale tomorrow!" answered Nasrudin.

Terrible Thirst

On his travels, the Mulla once spent the night at an inn where he received a warm welcome from the owner of the inn. "I am indeed delighted and honoured to have you here, O Mulla. If you need anything, anything at all, just call for it."

In the middle of the night the Mulla felt terribly thirsty. He called out for some water but no one heard him. He shouted for a long time, "Water, water!" but got no reply. He thought his mouth would burn up without water.

"Fire! Fire! FIRE!" he yelled.

Within minutes half the inn had burst into his room. The host himself stood near Nasrudin with a big pitcher of water. "Where is the fire, Mulla?" he asked.

"Right here!" said the Mulla, pointing to his mouth.

"Carrots"

The King sent Nasrudin to the East to learn about their mysticism. There, the Mulla met a number of mystics, of different kinds, who told him fascinating tales about miracles and the sayings of great men.

When he came back to his country, Nasrudin wrote out a report and submitted it. The report had just one word written on paper: "carrots".

The King demanded that Nasrudin explain what he meant by that. So the Mulla said, "What I learnt was that the best part of wisdom is buried and only a farmer can tell from the green leaves above the ground what lies underneath the soil. If you don't work to grow it, it will all be spoilt and go waste. And a lot of donkeys are running after it."

Meat-Pie

Nasrudin came home from the market with a smile on his face. He was muttering to himself and laughing.

"What is so funny?" his wife asked.

"I met a friend in the market who told me a new recipe for meat-pie. It sounded delicious so I wrote it down. And then I bought some meat as well so you could try out the recipe." Nasrudin replied.

"But why were you laughing about that?" asked his puzzled wife.

"That's not why I was laughing. On my way back a big bird swooped down and grabbed the meat out of my hand and flew off!"

"Oh no!" his wife exclaimed. "And you find that funny?" she asked.

"I tell you, these big birds. All feathers and no brains! It forgot to snatch the recipe from my other hand!"

31

Trust

A neighbour once asked Nasrudin if he could borrow his donkey. However, Nasrudin did not want to lend it out because the neighbour was a cruel and careless man. So he decided to lie.

"I am sorry, but someone has already borrowed my donkey for a week."

Just as Nasrudin was about to shut the door, the donkey brayed loudly from the backyard where it was tied.

The neighbour realised that the Mulla was trying to fool him. He said, "Shame on you for lying. I know your donkey is still here. I can hear it!"

Immediately Nasrudin banged the door shut on his neighbour's face, saying, "I will not lend anything to a man who believes in a donkey more than in what I have said!"

Lost and Found

The law of the kingdom was that anyone who found something on the street could not just keep it for himself. He must first go to the market place and shout out what he had found so that the original owner could come

and take it. If no one came even after three shouts, the man who found the object could keep it for himself.

One day, Nasrudin found a beautiful gold ring in the street. He wanted to keep it but he did not want to break the law.

In the middle of the night, people were woken up by a loud voice coming from the market; "I have found a gold ring on the street." The Mulla shouted this three times. By then, sleepy people had started to crowd around him.

"What did you say, Mulla?" they all asked him.

"Well, according to the law I am only supposed to say it three times, and I am a man who follows the rules. So I shall not say it again," replied Nasrudin. "But I can tell you this much, I am the owner of a beautiful gold ring!"

A Loyal Servant

Nasrudin was a great favourite with his king. One day he was entertaining the king in the court with his wit and wisdom when the king declared that he was very hungry.

That day the royal chef had cooked a very tasty meal of carrots. In his hunger, the king found them more delicious than usual. So he said that now he wished to eat carrots everyday.

"Aren't carrots the best vegetables, Nasrudin?" asked the king.

"Indeed, your Majesty, they are the very best vegetables in the whole world," replied Nasrudin.

After eating carrots for an entire week, the king was bored of the vegetable. He shouted, "I *hate* carrots. Never serve me carrots for a meal again!"

"They are the most tasteless vegetables in

the whole world, your Highness." Nasrudin agreed.

But the king was angry now. He glared at Nasrudin and said, "But only last week you said that they were the best vegetables! Make up your mind!"

Without blinking, the Mulla answered, "I did say so. But after all, your Highness, I am a servant to the king, not to the carrots!"

Borrowed Feathers Make Fine Birds

Jalal was an old friend of Nasrudin's who dropped in at his place one day. Nasrudin was just going out to visit a few people, so he asked Jalal to accompany him.

"I would like that," replied Jalal, "But I am not dressed well enough to go visiting. Lend me a coat, Nasrudin."

So Nasrudin lent Jalal one of the best coats he had. And then both of them set off.

At the first house they visited, Nasrudin introduced his friend. "This is my old friend, Jalal, but the coat he is wearing, that is mine."

On their way to the next house Jalal said, "That was such a silly thing to say, 'That coat is mine!' Don't do that again."

So at the next house Nasrudin introduced Jalal by saying, "This is Jalal, an old friend.

But his coat, that is not mine, it is *his*!" Poor Jalal was very embarrassed.

As they walked towards the next house he scolded Nasrudin. "What is wrong with you?"

"I am sorry," said Nasrudin, "I was just trying to make up for what I said at the first house."

"Well, why do you have to mention the robe at all?" said the exasperated Jalal.

When they reached the next house Nasrudin said, "Come meet my friend Jalal. He has come to visit me. And that coat he is wearing... but don't worry Jalal. I will not say anything about that coat!"

Run

Nasrudin was telling some friends the story of his trip through a lonely desert.

"You know," he said, "when I was in the desert I met a gang of dangerous Bedouins. They looked like they were going to kill me. But I made them run as fast as they could!"

"How on earth did you manage to do that?" they all asked wonderingly.

"Simple! When they saw me I ran like the wind and they all ran after me!"

A Good Host

One day Nasruddin sat bragging with a group of his friends. "There are few men more hospitable than I," he said.

His friends were quick to take him at his word. "Well then, take us to your home for a feast," they insisted.

Nasruddin led them towards his home but halfway there he said, "Let me at least warn my wife before all of you arrive at my doorstep." So he walked a little faster and reached his house before them.

His wife got really angry when she heard what he had done and shouted, "There is no food in the house for people to come and eat whenever they want. Tell them to go away."

But Nasrudin had already promised them a feast. And now he was scared to tell them to leave. They would laugh at him or get angry. They might even call him a liar. So his wife agreed to send everyone away by saying that he was not at home.

After waiting outside Nasruddin's house for a really long time, the men began shouting to be let in. His wife came out onto the balcony and said, "My husband is not here. He will be back late."

But the crowd did not believe her. "We saw him go in, didn't we? How can he have left without us seeing him?"

The wife did not know what to say. She kept quiet. But now Nasruddin, who had heard all the shouting, could take it no more. He leant out of the window near his hiding place and yelled, "You fools! I could have left the house by the back door, couldn't I?"

Fifty-Fifty

After a lot of difficulty Nasrudin managed to gain entry into the Royal Court as he had some good news to share with the king. Once he had announced the news, the king thanked him warmly.

"That is indeed good news, Mulla. Thank you for bringing it to me. What reward do you want in return for this?"

"Your Majesty, I would like to receive fifty lashes."

The whole court was filled with the buzzing voices of the puzzled courtiers. Whoever heard of a man demanding lashes as a reward? They started eyeing the Mulla suspiciously, thinking that he was a little crazy.

"Nasrudin, I asked you what reward you wanted. What sort of an answer is that?" said the king.

"Your Highness," said the Mulla, "I had to

bribe the guard at the palace gates in order to get in here today. He made me promise that I would share with him whatever I get as a reward—fifty-fifty. Otherwise he refused to let me in. So after I receive my twenty-five lashes you can call him in and give him his fair share of the lashings!"